Sam Goes Trucking

Sam Goes Trucking

Henry Horenstein

Houghton Mifflin Company

Boston

This book is for Evan.

Library of Congress Cataloging-in-Publication Data

Horenstein, Henry.
  Sam goes trucking.
  Summary: Sam spends the day with his trucker father in a sixteen-wheeler.
  ISBN 0-395-44313-X
  [1. Truck driving—Fiction] I. Title.
PZ7.H7809Sam 1989   88-8321
[E]

Printed in the United States of America

RNF ISBN 0-395-44313-X
PAP ISBN 0-395-54950-7

WOZ 10 9 8 7

This is Sam. He's sitting in his dad's Mack truck, model R-600. Today Sam and his dad are going trucking together.

It's six A.M. Truckers have to get up early and eat a healthy breakfast.
They have a long day ahead of them.

"Where are we heading, Dad?"

"To the pier to pick up a load of fish. Then we'll head north to take the load to the market."

First they go to the truck terminal.

"The fish must be kept cold, Sam, so we'll be using the reefer today.

That's what we call the refrigerator trailer."

"Before we leave we'd better look at the map to find the best route."

Sam and his dad give the Mack a thorough checkup to make sure it's safe for the road.

Now it's time to hitch the trailer to the cab.

The electrical cord, called the pigtail, is hooked up so the trailer's lights will work.
Then the air hoses are attached for the trailer's brake.

The trailer won't budge until the landing gear is lifted.

"When you finish cranking, Sam, yell 'dolly up' and I'll know we're ready to move."

The inside of the Mack's cab has everything a car has and more.

The shift is used constantly to change gears.

Because of this, truckers are sometimes called gear jammers.

14

Truckers use the CB to talk about weather conditions and traffic and just to pass the time. Sam's dad's call handle is Big Stuff.
"I think my handle should be Little Stuff, Dad."

Before they hit the road, they have to put air in the tires, check the oil, and have the tank filled with diesel fuel.

This Mack has eighteen wheels, so truckers call it an eighteen-wheeler.

Finally they're off.

The white lines on the road mark the traveling lanes. When truckers get tired, they say they have white-line fever.

At the pier the fish are taken from the boats, packed in crates, and then wheeled into the reefer.

"This Mack can haul a lot of fish, Sam. Fully loaded, it can pull fifty-thousand pounds."

Soon they are on the road again.

"Dad, I'm starving. Let's get lunch."

"Good idea. I know just the place—Cindy's Truck Stop."

"Hey, Dad. That truck up ahead just honked his horn at us."
"That's Joe Marsh. I'll bet he's headed for Cindy's too."

"Come on, Sam.
Let's get some burgers and fries."

"Look at all these trucks, Dad. That's a Kenworth, isn't it?"

They sit at the counter with the other truckers.

"How's it going, Rose? This is my son Sam. He's riding with me today."

After lunch they do a quick check of the oil and are ready to hit the road again.

"Are we almost there, Dad?"
"We're right at the city limits now, Sam."

Backing up a large trailer with a full load takes a lot of skill.

The forklift is great for unloading the fish. This is much faster than unloading by hand.

"Want to help me fill out the log, Sam?"
The log provides a record of how many miles a truck travels and where it goes.

"Let's push this diesel back home, Sam."
"Good idea, but what's that siren, Dad?"

32

"Oh, no! That's a smokey, Sam. We've got to pull over."

"What's a smokey, Dad?"

"That's what truckers call a state trooper."

34

"Hello. This is just a routine safety check. May I see your license, registration, and trip log, please?"

The trooper checks the papers, and everything is in order.

"Whew! I thought he had us there, Sam."

"Good thing you always stick to the speed limit, Dad, or we'd be in big trouble."

Back on the road again. Their hometown is almost in sight.

It has been a long day for Sam, but you can bet he will be out trucking again very soon.

Thanks to everyone who helped with this book: Ruth Glicksman, Jan Sahlstrom, Charles and Eric Nunes and the workers at Sea View Fillet Company, especially Mark Jardin, John Ramos, and Michael Soares. Thanks to Richard Palermo of the B&M Fish Company, to Colonel Walter E. Stone, Captain John T. Leyden, Jr., Captain Frank McGee, Sergeant Harry Speight, Trooper John LaFreniere, and Trooper Raymond White, of the Rhode Island State Police Department, Melissa Tardiff, D-Fillet Company, and to Susan Sherman and Walter Lorraine at Houghton Mifflin. Special thanks to Evan Sahlstrom and David Glicksman.